This
Korky Paul
PICTURE BOOK
BELONGS TO:

_____

_____

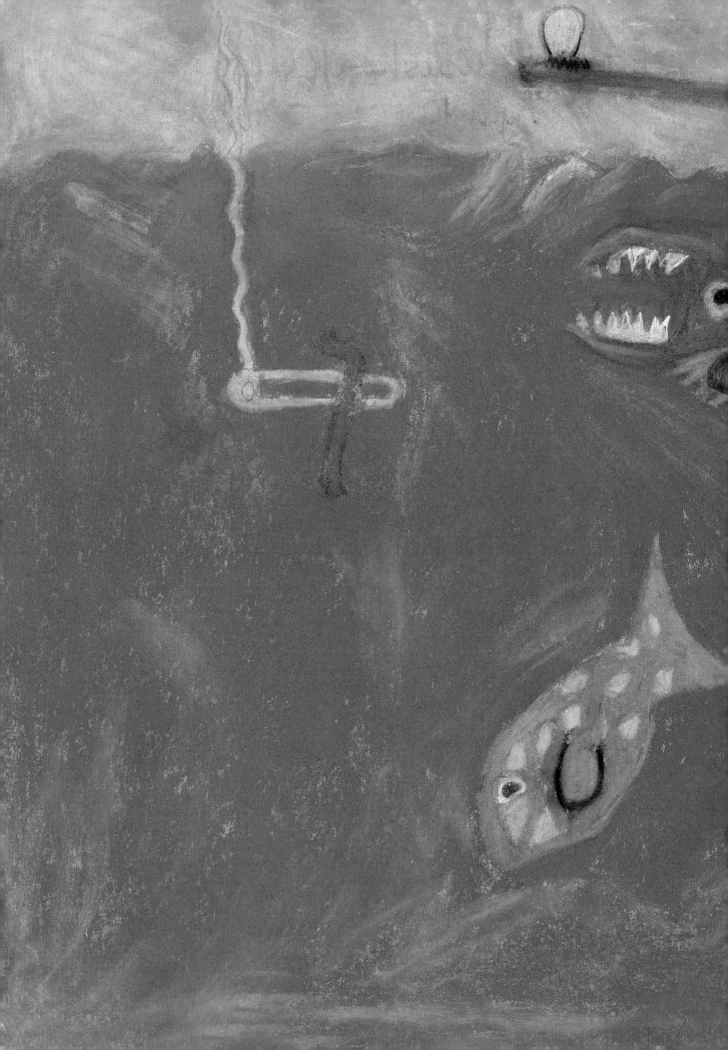

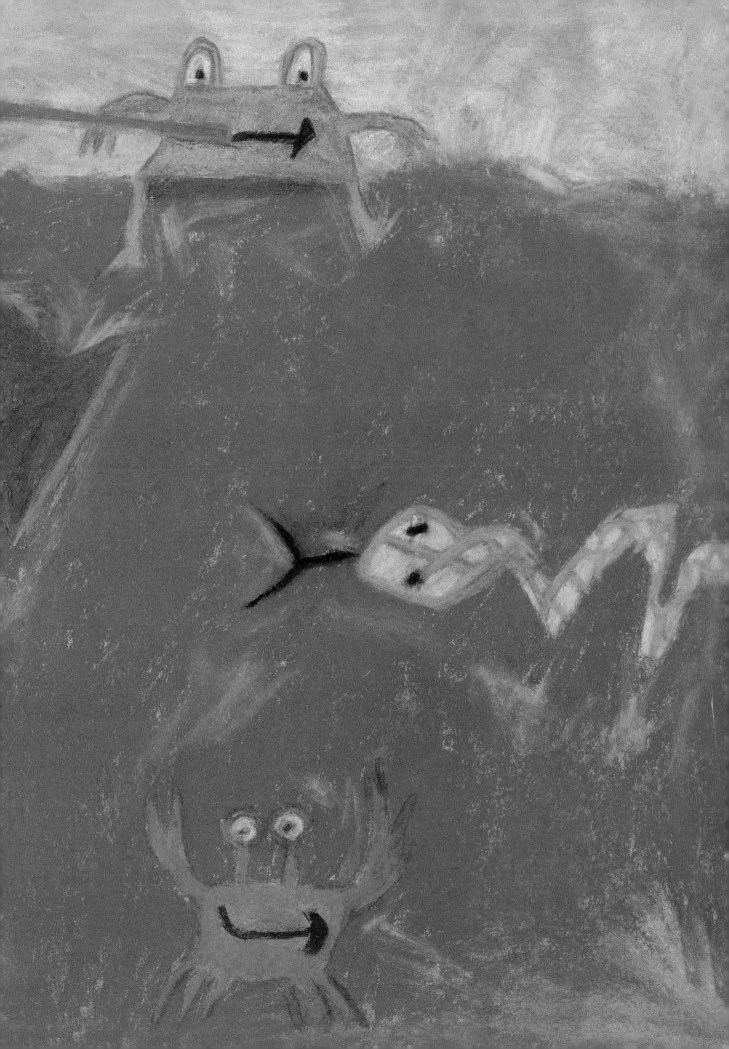

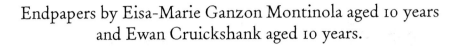

Endpapers by Eisa-Marie Ganzon Montinola aged 10 years
and Ewan Cruickshank aged 10 years.

A big thank you to New Marston Primary School, Oxford
for helping with the endpapers – K.P.

For my son John – R.T.
For Tom Stoffer – K.P.

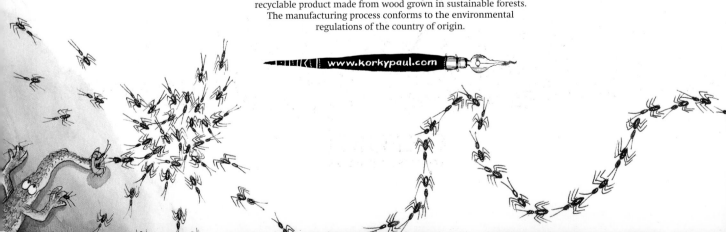

OXFORD
UNIVERSITY PRESS

Great Clarendon Street, Oxford OX2 6DP
Oxford University Press is a department of the University of Oxford.
It furthers the University's objective of excellence in research, scholarship,
and education by publishing worldwide in

Oxford New York

Auckland Cape Town Dar es Salaam Hong Kong Karachi
Kuala Lumpur Madrid Melbourne Mexico City Nairobi
New Delhi Shanghai Taipei Toronto

With offices in

Argentina Austria Brazil Chile Czech Republic France Greece
Guatemala Hungary Italy Japan Poland Portugal Singapore
South Korea Switzerland Thailand Turkey Ukraine Vietnam

www.korkypaul.com

When Chico Went Fishing

Written by Robin Tzannes

OXFORD

UNIVERSITY PRESS

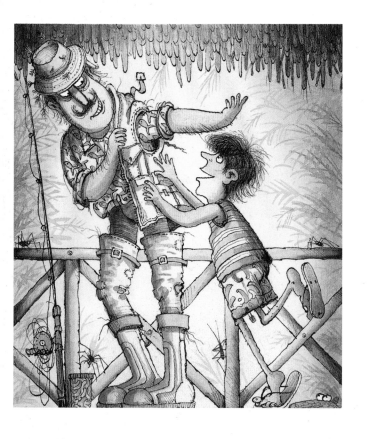

One day Chico's father was going fishing.

'Oh, Daddy, may I come too?' asked Chico. 'Please, Daddy? *Please*?'

His father shook his head. 'No, son. You're too young. You'll talk too much and scare away the fish. You'll fidget and fuss and get in the way.' But, seeing the tears in Chico's eyes, he patted his head gently. 'Maybe when you're older . . .'

Then he picked up his fishing tackle and set off.

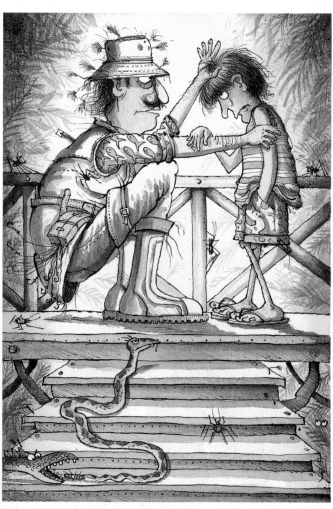

Chico went for a walk. He felt sad. 'I *am* old enough to go fishing!' he thought. 'I would sit quietly. I wouldn't scare the fish! And I wouldn't get in the way!'

He kept on walking, and soon he reached the river. That gave him an idea. 'I *will* go fishing!' he said. 'All by myself. Then they'll see!'

Chico climbed onto a big rock and looked down into the river. He could see the little fish swimming in the water. But how could he catch one? 'First, I'll need a fishing rod,' he decided.

So he went into the woods and searched for a stick that looked just right and very soon he found one.

He brought it back to the big
rock. Chico sat down and held
the stick out over the water.
He waited. And waited.

Nothing happened.

At last he remembered
something. 'Line!' shouted
Chico. 'Of course, I need
a line!'

Now, Chico was the kind of boy whose pockets were always full of interesting things.

He emptied them now, and found: a half-eaten sandwich, two buttons, a red pencil, part of a broken alarm clock, a shell, three marbles, some crumpled paper, a rusted toy car, a pebble . . . and a tangle of string. This he untangled, and tied onto his stick. Then he let the string dangle in the water.

Chico waited patiently.

Sometimes the little fish would swim up to the string, sniff at it, and swim away. How were they ever to get *caught*?

Chico thought and thought, until he had the answer. 'Hook!' he shouted. 'I need a hook on the end of the string!'

Now, Chico was the kind of boy who was always tearing his clothes. And most of the time, there were safety pins holding things together. He quickly checked his shirt, and then his shorts.

Sure enough, in the hem of his shorts, was a shiny safety pin. Chico bent the pin into the shape of a hook. Then he tied it onto his string, and let it drop into the water.

Chico sat down quietly and waited. The little fish darted in and out of the river weeds, but they hardly seemed to notice the hook.

While Chico watched them he began to wonder: how could he make them bite the hook?

And then he remembered. 'Worms! Fish *love* worms!'

Now, Chico was the kind of boy who was especially good at finding worms.

He ran quickly into the woods and began turning over rocks. Soon he had a fistful of pink and juicy worms.

He chose the biggest, most delicious looking one, and very carefully put it onto his hook. Then he lowered it into the water.

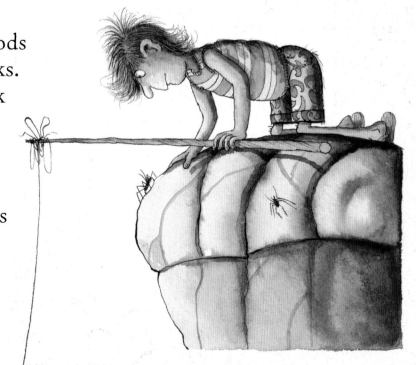

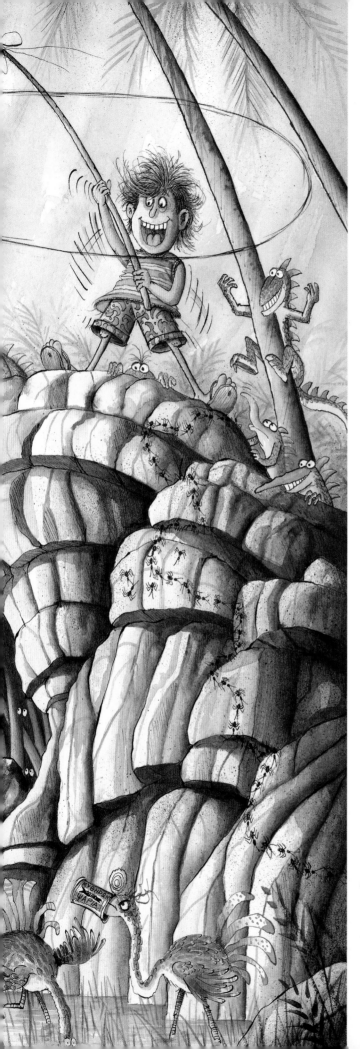

Sure enough, the little fish began sniffing the worm. But suddenly they all darted away, when a big, fat, green-spotted fish swam into view.

The big fish sniffed and sniffed . . . and then . . . he chomped down on the worm – hook, line and all!

The big fish was heavy, but Chico held on tight and pulled it out of the water. 'I *knew* I could catch a fish!' he cried.

Then he set off for home, feeling very happy.

When Chico got home he shouted, 'Mummy, Mummy, come and look at this fish!'

'My, that is *big*!' said his mother. 'Did Daddy catch it?'

'No,' smiled Chico.

'Well, then, who gave it to you?'

'Nobody!' replied Chico.

His mother was puzzled. 'You couldn't have found that fish . . .'

'Nope,' answered Chico.

'Then where on earth . . ?' his mother began.

'I caught it!' cried Chico. 'All by myself. And oh, Mummy, isn't it *beautiful*?'

Soon Chico's father came home.
He hadn't caught a single fish.

When he saw Chico's big fat fish,
he was amazed.

Chico told him the whole story.

'Chico,' said his father, 'you are
a natural-born fisherman! I'd
love to see how you do it. Will
you take me with you, next time
you go fishing?'

'I don't know,' said Chico. 'You
might talk and scare away the fish.'

'No,' said his father, 'I won't.'

'Will you fidget and fuss?' asked
Chico. 'And get in the way?'

'No,' said his father. 'I promise.'

'Well,' said Chico. 'I guess you're
old enough . . .'

Then he started to giggle, and
his father did too.

'Yes, Daddy!' laughed Chico.
'I'll be *happy* to take you with
me, next time I go fishing!'

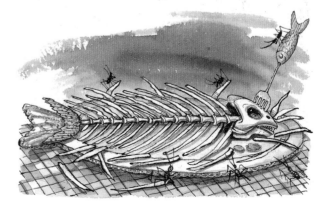

www.korkypaul.com